THIS BOOK BELONGS TO

----

MY FAVOURITE POEM IS

----

# **A**LPHABETICAL **P**OETICAL - 2

**Steve Morley** was born in Bradford in Yorkshire. He had a number of different jobs before becoming a trainee teacher. He reluctantly abandoned teaching training to become a champion chicken slaughterer for which he was given the nickname Claudius, because 'he murdered most foul'. After a short spell in uniform, with Bradford City Transport, he left for the bright lights of London to pursue a career as an actor, a profession that has intermittently entertained him for more than forty years.

For over a decade Steve played Sergeant Lamont in TV's ever popular *The Bill* (for which he also worked as a script writer); this was a part he was eternally grateful for as he appeared so infrequently no-one ever recognised him. But forget the world tours of great Shakespearean roles, forget the trip to Hollywood, forget even fighting Cybermen and being the vet in *Emmerdale*, Steve still regards his greatest claim to fame as winning an award for being the first man to appear nude on Irish radio.

In 2006 Steve was nominated for the national award of Teacher of the Year.

In 2010 *The Nutting Plays* and *The Farmhouse Plays* were nominated for a Company of Educators' Award.

In 2020 Steve retired from teaching at the City of London School for Girls where he had been Director of Drama for twenty years.

*By the same author*

## *For Adults*

*Novels*

TALES FROM THE TAP ROOM
SCREEN TEST
THE MIRACLE OF SNECKIT
ZORBA THE IRISH
THE NAP

*Short Stories*

SHEPPERTON: THE OUTWARD JOURNEY
SHEPPERTON: THE RETURN JOURNEY

*Plays*

STEVE MORLEY: PLAYS

## *For Children*

*Plays*

THE FARMHOUSE PLAYS
THE NUTTING PLAYS
THE COMPLETE NUTTING PAYS

*Verse*

ALPHABETICAL POETICAL - 1
ALPHABETICAL POETICAL - 2
ALPHABETICAL POETICAL - 3

# ALPHABETICAL POETICAL - 2

## by Steve Morley

## More humorous verse for kids

**ALPHABETICAL POETICAL - 2**
© Steve Morley 2021

**CONDITION OF SALE**

This book is sold subject to the condition that it shall not, by way of trade or otherwise, be lent, re-sold, hired out or otherwise circulated in any form of binding or cover other than that which it is published and without a similar condition including this condition being imposed on the subsequent purchaser.

**ALL ENQUIRIES**

**mrsteve.morley@outlook.com**

*For Thalia and Theo…*

*…and with thanks to Jo Russell and Jenny Brown*

A

## A

A is a letter that's very hard of hearing,
In fact, it's deaf, you really have to say.
For if you were to ask it, to tell you what it's called,
The letter A will always answer, "Eh?"

~ ~ ~ ~ ~

## Absolutely Totally

Absolutely, totally,
Thoroughly through and through,
I understand that forty-two
Is twenty-one times two.

Absolutely, totally,
Thoroughly through and through,
I understand that G-N-U
Spells out the word gnu.

Absolutely, totally,
Thoroughly through and through,
I understand that trillions
Will never be a few.

Absolutely, totally,
Thoroughly through and through,
I understand that sailing ships
Will sink without a crew.

Absolutely, totally,
Thoroughly through and through,
I understand that red and green
Won't make the colour blue.

Absolutely, totally,
Thoroughly through and through,
I understand a liar can't
Promise something true.

Absolutely, totally,
Thoroughly through and through,
I understand there are some days
I do not have a clue.

Absolutely, totally,
Thoroughly through and through,
I understand that doing nowt
Will leave a lot to do.

Absolutely, totally,
Thoroughly through and through,
I understand that every day
I'm learning something new.

Absolutely, totally,
Thoroughly through and through,
I understand that I'm just me,
Thoroughly, through and through.

~ ~ ~ ~ ~

## **A**lfonso Faylin

Alfonso Faylin found he was ailing,
So he went to the doctor's house.
Alfonso found the doctor wailing,
So he was treated by his spouse.

Alfonso Faylin then went out sailing,
That's how he earned his daily bread.
Alfonso took the spouse's kaolin,
And that's how he came to be dead.

~ ~ ~ ~ ~

Steve Morley	Alphabetical Poetical – 2

# B

## **B**ananas

Bananas are a silly fruit
Which bend in a curious way
More like a boomerang than a flute
With a taste that's hard to say.
But try to throw one through the sky,
It won't fly back this way,
And if you want to give it a try,
It's a devilish thing to play.

~ ~ ~ ~ ~

## **B**lack **B**oomerang

Never throw a boomerang
If it is coloured black,
Especially at night for you'll
Not see it coming back.

~ ~ ~ ~ ~

## **Bear Rings**

I have a little circus act,
A company of bears.
We like to train throughout the Spring
When they have left their lairs.

In circles they all like to dance,
Around and round they go,
With spinning shapes and pirouettes,
A dizzy-making show.

But then I always lose them all,
I don't know where they go,
I'm always losing my bear rings,
That's why there is no show.

~ ~ ~ ~ ~

Steve Morley        Alphabetical Poetical – 2

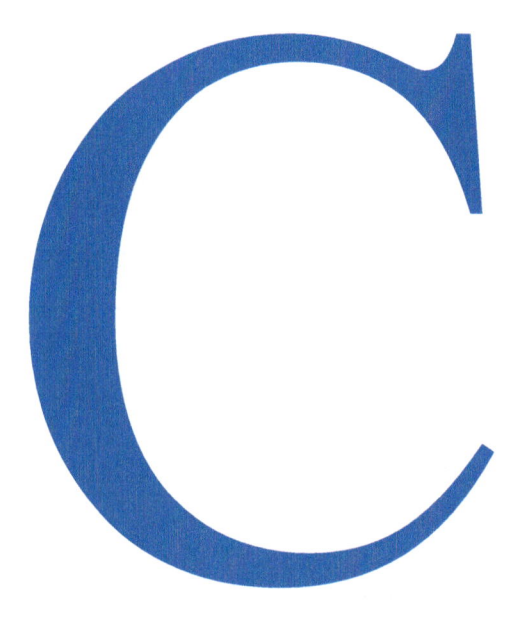

C

## **C**ollie

My sheepdog is a collie
He's very old and hobbles.
He rests his belly
On plates of jelly
Then gets the collywobbles!

~ ~ ~ ~ ~

## **C**onundrum

When I was young, not that long ago,
I joined up to a marching band.
I would march along, with tune and song,
A conundrum safe in my hand.

Whatever it was, this conundrum,
I never ever did find out.
But its deafening sound was so loud,
If you heard it, you had to shout.

Upon one day, it just disappeared,
And I lost my conundrum friend.
Wherever it went, I'll never know,
A conundrum right to the end.

~ ~ ~ ~ ~

## **C**uddly Toys?

At first it was a polar bear,
Ba-Ba was his name,
And then there was a dinosaur,
Who I called Bronto-Brain.
Next to arrive was Daffy Duck,
Then there came a dog,
And after that arrived a goose,
Soon followed by a frog.

And when at last my birthday came,
More of them arrived,
Three birds, a teddy, and a horse,
Were wrapped and so supplied.
At Christmas came a carload,
Dozens of the things,
Squeaky ones and some that burp
And one that smiles and sings.

They're all placed on my bed at night,
Just for me to see
Them sitting there. But pretty soon,
There'll be no room for me.

~ ~ ~ ~ ~

Steve Morley Alphabetical Poetical – 2

# D

## Debating

Debating is a wonderful thing,
You can get a lot out of it.
At school, I wished it to be my thing
But then I was talked out of it.

~ ~ ~ ~ ~

## Dolorous

There was a young girl called Dolorous,
Whose skin was all holey and porous,
She was in a play,
And earned lots of pay,
By playing a sponge in the chorus.

~ ~ ~ ~ ~

## **D**olphin

I once made friends with a dolphin,
Down by a southern sea.
And we would play out in the bay,
Then he'd come home for tea.

We'd spend many hours together,
Among the waves we'd picked,
And through the day, within the bay,
Me and the dolphin clicked.

He asked if I would like to swim
With him on the seabed.
But I think I need that like I
Need a hole in the head!

~~~~~

Steve Morley                    Alphabetical Poetical – 2

# E

## **Easy-Peasy**

Sailing is a lovely thing
Though it can make you queasy
But when at last you get it right
It's oh so easy-peasy

Gliding is a graceful thing
Especially when it's breezy
But when at last you float on high
It feels so easy-peasy

Breathing is a natural thing
Though not if you are wheezy
But when you do it without thought
It's ever so easy-peasy

Cooking is a handy thing
That can be very greasy
But when your dishes turn out right
It seems so easy-peasy

Writing verse – now there's a thing
That can be very cheesy
But when it's right – it's sheer delight
Though rarely easy-peasy.

~ ~ ~ ~ ~

# Eggs

> There is a deliberate mistake in this verse. Can you spot it? Answer at the top of page 18.

Eggs have no legs,
    They can't run round,
        They spend their lives
            Upon the ground.
Eggs have no backs,
    They cannot stretch
        Aching muscles
            Within their necks.
Eggs cannot swim,
    Unlike kippers,
        In the water,
            They've no flippers
Eggs have no feet,
    They stay in line,
        When it comes to
            Breakfast time
Eggs have no eyes
    They cannot see
        Me with soldiers,
            Egg cup and tea.
So pity the egg,
    When you dip its yolk,
        Eggs cannot laugh,
            And that's no joke!

~ ~ ~ ~ ~

## **Easy-Peasy (2)**

If you pick up a peapod
And press it on the seam
Then hey diddle-diddle
It splits down the middle
Revealing the peas in between

~ ~ ~ ~ ~

> *EGGS* - DELIBERATE MISTAKE
>
> Kippers can't swim either!

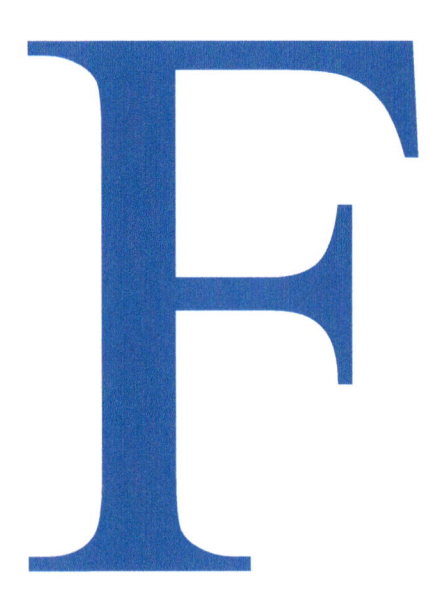

# F

## Fishes With the Dishes

There are fishes with the dishes,
How on earth did they get there?
They're in the sink, I cannot think,
They appeared out of thin air.

There are fishes washing dishes,
They just flick them with their tails.
I must confess, there'd be a mess,
If they'd not been fish but whales!

I'm so thankful for this tankful,
I could give them all a hug,
But I'll just sigh, and say goodbye,
After I pull out the plug.

~ ~ ~ ~ ~

## Failed Poem

I'm going to write a poem
That will not have a rhyme,
But it will be a failure 'cos
I rhyme things all the time.

~ ~ ~ ~ ~

## **Forgetful Anteater**

The anteater stopped in the jungle,
And paused as he tried to recall,
Just why he was in such a bungle,
What was he to do there at all?

Now was it for jam or for treacle,
That he had come out for this walk?
Or was it to meet up with people,
To speak of the weather and talk?

Or was it for getting of porridge,
Or just for a walk in the park?
He surely had lost all his knowledge,
Oh dear, what a silly aardvark.

The anteater thought as he grumbled,
And scratched with a foot at his pants,
And then he looked down and he mumbled,
And remembered the reason: Ants!

~ ~ ~ ~ ~

Steve Morley  Alphabetical Poetical – 2

G

## **Get Up and Go**

While lazing round the house one day
My mother said to me,
"Where's your get up and go, young man,
Where is your energy?

"You can't sit there all day," she said,
"It's lazy and it's wrong!"
But what if your get up and go
Has just got up and gone?

I looked at her in disbelief,
I knew just what she meant,
But what if your get up and go
Had just stood up and went?

She really was quite angry now,
And I would have copped it,
So I found my get up and go,
Jumped right up and hopped it!

~ ~ ~ ~ ~

## Grandad

My Grandad says, 'Don't pick your nose!'
I like that!
He picks his nose, in the car waiting at traffic lights.
It's true.

My Grandad says, 'Don't play with your food!'
I like that!
He plays with his, even if it is under his teeth.
It's true.

My Grandad says, 'You'll never grow up strong!'
I like that!
I'm not so weak I have to go to sleep on Sundays
after the pub.
It's true.

My Grandad says, 'You'll get square eyes!'
I like that!
I suppose he means like he has when he puts his
glasses on.
It's true.

My Grandad says, 'Go ask your Grandmother!'
I like that!
She says he never tells her about anything.
It's true.

My Grandad says, 'Speak when you're spoken to!'
I like that!
In that case how can I ask Grandmother anything?
It's true.

My Grandad says, 'You have to eat your greens!'
Oh, I really like that!
I suppose he means like he does at traffic lights.
It's true!

~ ~ ~ ~ ~

## Garry The Biscuit

Garry wants his hair cut,
But doesn't want to risk it.
He thinks because he's very old
He'll end up like a biscuit.
I said, "Garry, it's perfectly safe,
Even though you are an oldie."
But he replied, "If they shave my head,
I'll be a Garry-baldi."

~ ~ ~ ~ ~

Steve Morley  Alphabetical Poetical – 2

H

## Hoarder

I'm going to have to stockpile
Some food for thirty days.
I'll keep it in the freezer,
No matter what mum says.

I'll be hoarding lots of ice-cream,
Raspberry sauce and fruit,
And maybe some milk chocolate bits,
(I do not care a hoot).

I wanted to do this quickly,
But now I'm not so sure,
For after a month of sundaes,
I'll not get through the door!

~~~~~

## Horse

I met a horse the other day
Out looking for his voice,
He didn't often come this way
It seems he had no choice.
What can you say to such a nag
Who offers no recourse,
Except for you to tell and brag
You've met a hoarsey horse.

~~~~~

## How Do You Solve the Problem of the Poet?

There is an old poet called Morley,
Whose brains always ache rather sorely.
He tries all the time
To find words that rhyme,
But he can't, and that makes him ill.

~ ~ ~ ~ ~

*WHAT IS THE ANSWER TO THE QUESTION?*

*HOW WOULD YOU HELP THE OLD POET?*

Steve Morley  Alphabetical Poetical – 2

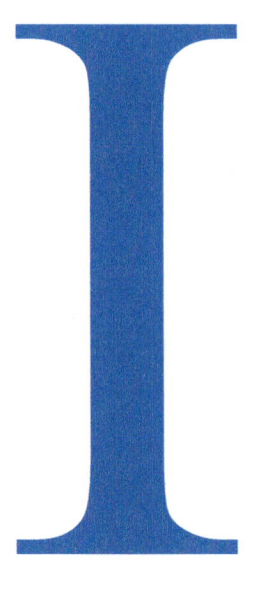

I

## Ice Cream

The ice cream suddenly flew into the air,
Don't ask me why, it was just like a dream.
The ice cream suddenly splattered on my hair
Don't ask me how, but I didn't half scream.

Ice cream in the air and I scream,
Ice cream on my hair and I scream.
I scream, "Ice cream,"
"Ice cream," I scream.

Ice cream in my hair
Why wasn't it a dream?

~ ~ ~ ~ ~

## If I Were A Magnet

If I were a magnet
I'd be so interactive,
Then everyone I chance to meet
Would say I'm most attractive.

~ ~ ~ ~ ~

## I Used To Know

I used to know a hedgehog,
Who was known to all as Mikey,
And said he'd never wash his hair
Because it came out spikey.

I used to know a mammal,
Who was a seaside rotter,
And said he never went indoors
Because it made him otter.

I used to know a kangaroo,
Who was so very grumpy,
And said he never liked the dark
Because it made him jumpy.

I used to know a crocodile,
Who was so very happy,
But wildebeest he never liked
Because they made him snappy.

I used to know a rabbit,
Who was a little poppet,
But said she never liked being chased
Because she had to hop it.

I used to know a racehorse,
Who had a toothy grin,
And if he never brushed his teeth
He'd hardly ever win.

I used to know a teacher,
Who gave me lots to do,
And I thought if I got my way,
I'd flush him down the loo!

This teacher came right up to me,
And told me I was good,
Now if I ever get the chance
I tell the neighbourhood.

I now know lots of creatures,
They're all a bit like me,
Do you think that we will ever know
How silly we can be?

~ ~ ~ ~ ~

Steve Morley    Alphabetical Poetical – 2

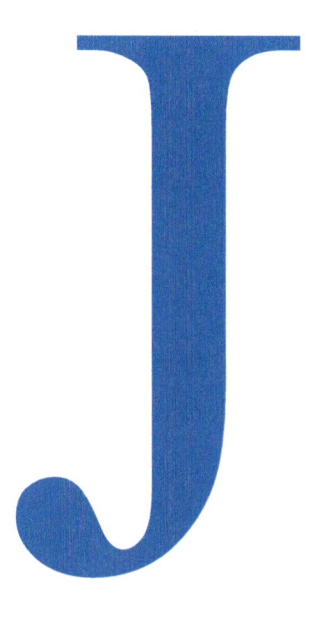

J

## Jippetty-Jappetty-Jumpetty

Jippetty-Jappetty-Jumpetty-jot,
He knows what I haven't got.
Jippetty-Jappetty-Jumpetty-joo,
He knows what you've not got too.

Jippetty-Jappetty-Jumpetty-jee,
He knows what's not owned by me.
Jippetty-Jappetty-Jumpetty-jell,
He knows what's not yours as well.

Jippetty-Jappetty-Jumpetty-jink,
He knows what I think I think.
Jippetty-Jappetty-Jumpetty-jo,
He knows what you think I know.

Jippetty-Jappetty-Jumpetty-jed,
He knows it's not what I said.
Jippetty-Jappetty-Jumpetty-jold,
He knows it's not what you told.

Jippetty-Jappetty-Jumpetty-jom,
Came to see where he came from,
Jippetty-Jappetty-Jumpetty-jay,
Found he'd left and gone away.

Jippetty-Jappetty-Jumpetty-jense,
He makes sense of all nonsense.
Jippetty-Jappetty-Jumpetty-jy,
Nonsense makes sense if you try.

~ ~ ~ ~ ~

## **Jack And Jill**

Jack and Jill and a boy named Bill,
Were playing upon a rafter,
Bill fell on his head and was quite dead,
And the twins were filled with laughter.

Jack and Jill and a boy called Will,
Were cooking vegetable pies,
The food was off, and then, with a cough,
Will falls to the floor and he dies.

Jack and Jill and a girl named Lill,
Were playing at making bread,
The flour went whirl and so did the girl
And ground her until she was dead.

Jack and Jill and a boy named Phil,
Were playing at hide and seek,
Phil then hid away and to this day,
He hasn't been seen for a week.

Jack and Jill and a girl called Till,
Were whirling around and around,
The twins let go, Till fell in the snow,
And has never, not ever, been found.

Jack and Jill took some kids and a drill,
And made a terrible mess,
They were laid on coals and filled with holes,
And what happened next you can guess.

Jack and Jill went up the hill,
To fetch a pail of water,
Jill looked down, upon the town,
And shrieked at all the slaughter.

~~~~~

## **Jittery Jack**

Jittery Jack had quite a knack
For falling on his back.
But as he walked the tightrope
He very soon got the sack.

~~~~~

Steve Morley         Alphabetical Poetical – 2

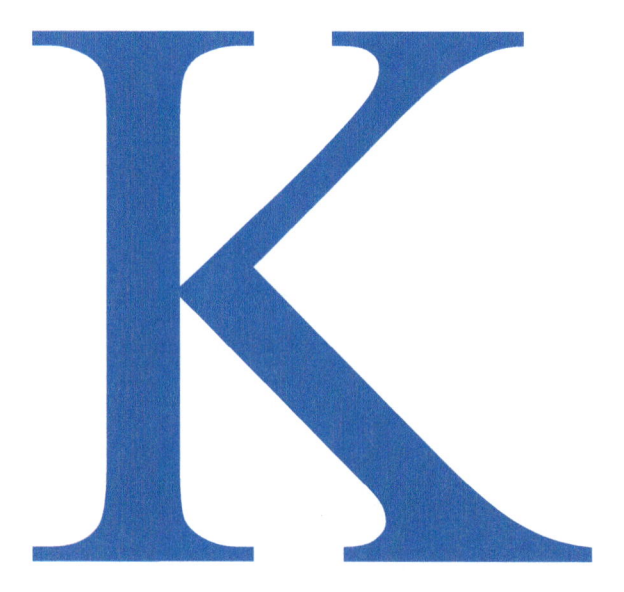

K

## Ketteledrum

My kettledrum is famous,
A very well-known thing,
For when it's on the gas stove
It begins to sing.

My kettledrum is magic,
The finest you could see,
For when I bang upon it,
It makes a cup of tea

~~~~~

## Kelvin and Melvin

There once was a young lad called Kelvin,
Whose one-legged brother was Melvin.
His hatred was such
That he'd kick Melvin's crutch,
And what else he did we won't delve in.

~~~~~

## Kilometre

Could you ever kilometre?
I don't think that I could,
Because I think a metre holds
An awful lot of blood.

~~~~~

Steve Morley    Alphabetical Poetical – 2

L

## **Little Mary's Prayer**

God in Heaven please listen,
I've not asked since You know when,
But do me this one favour,
And I will not ask again.

The first night could be awful,
My parents will both be there,
My Grandma will bring Grandad,
And really I do not care

If I mess up all my words,
And trample on Joseph's toes,
And bash into the shepherds
And tangle with Herod's clothes,

And trip up all the angels.
I do not care who sees us.
But dearest God in Heaven,
Don't let me drop Your Jesus.

~ ~ ~ ~ ~

## Laughing Cavalier

What has he got to laugh about, that laughing Cavalier?
Did he just catch a Roundhead and kick him in the rear?
Or did King Charles just ring him up to take him for a beer?
Just what's he got to grin about, that laughing cavalier?

What has he got to smirk about, that laughing Cavalier?
Did he just take a Roundhead and make him quake in fear?
Or did the National Theatre say he's needed for King Lear?
Just what's he got to smile about, that laughing Cavalier?

Why does he seem to chortle so, that laughing Cavalier?
Did he just grab a Roundhead and smack him in the ear?
Or has he won a raffle worth a thousand pounds a year?
Just what's he got laugh about, that laughing Cavalier?

What has he creased his mug about, that laughing Cavalier?
Did he just see a Roundhead all dressed up in women's gear?
Or did he hear that Cromwell just fell down from Brighton pier?
Oh what's he so damned smug about that laughing Cavalier?

~ ~ ~ ~ ~

## Lance

My name is Lance.
It's a very unpopular name.
It's a name that seems to have been forgot.
Poor old Lance!
But back in King Arthur's times
Parents called their children Lance a lot.

~ ~ ~ ~ ~

Steve Morley       Alphabetical Poetical – 2

# M

## Mister McGrew

Mister McGrew went to the zoo
And because he was thin, they kept him in.
Yes, he was thin, he wasn't thick,
So they called him an insect and named him Stick

~ ~ ~ ~ ~

## Mona Lisa's Dad

Mona Lisa's dear old father
Said unto her one day,
"I've found you a decent job, dear,
You'll really like the pay.
It is posing for an artist,
He has your name on file,
But you'll never keep it, girl,
If you don't learn to smile."

~ ~ ~ ~ ~

## Mother's Ruin

Mother's really told me off,
She gave me quite a drubbing,
But how can I scrub behind my ears
When I can't see what I'm scrubbing?

Mother's had another go,
I've never heard such language,
But how can I grow up big and strong,
When she makes me eat boiled cabbage?

Mother's told me off again,
I've never had as many,
But how on earth do I pull up socks,
When I'm not wearing any?

Mother's shouting up the stairs,
In a voice that's doom and gloom,
But how will I not get very far,
If I don't clean my bedroom?

Mother's shouting out once more,
She's asking what I'm doing.
I'm sulking, because I don't know why
I'm going to be her ruin.

~ ~ ~ ~ ~

Steve Morley    Alphabetical Poetical – 2

N

## Nelly The Elephant

Nelly the elephant packed her trunk
And said goodbye to the circus,
A rubber trumpet she had found
And played it oh, so grand,
And now she searches everywhere
To find a rubber band.

~ ~ ~ ~ ~

## Nic

There was a young lady called Nic,
Who tended to speak rather quick,
And talk fast she could,
So none understood,
Which made them all think she was thick.

~ ~ ~ ~ ~

## **Nobody's Fools (A Song)**
*(Readers are invited to create their own music for this song.)*

       Terry loves our Lucy,
       Sue's in love with Biff,
       Dennis doesn't love anyone at all,
       Except perhaps Miss Smith.
       Miss Smith is our teacher,
       She rides a motorbike,
       Sheila thinks it's dangerous,
       And so does little Mike...Oh!

       *Chorus*:

*Singing a song about Class A Eleven,*
*Singing a song about the worst of schools,*
*We are the class of twenty-seven.*
*But we'll turn out nobody's fools.*
    *(Clap-clap, clap)*
*No, we'll turn out nobody's fools.*

       The seniors think they're better,
       We know better than that,
       You need to have a very big head
       To fit in a very big hat.
       We see them out at playtime,
       They think they're so smart,
       But we've made a very big bomb
       And we'll blow them all apart...Oh!

       *Chorus*

Dennis is a whizz-kid,
He deals with T.N.T.,
He makes Guy Fawkes look like a shepherd
In the Nativity.
He's been through all the cellars,
This kid is not dumb.
And come next week we'll blow them all
Right to kingdom come...Oh!

*Chorus*

Tuesday is our day off,
We're going on a tour,
Down to the Houses of Parliament,
See how they rule the poor.
We'll learn all our lessons,
Each of us a gem,
And when we leave the school quite soon,
We're coming back for them...Oh!

*Chorus*

~ ~ ~ ~ ~

Steve Morley					Alphabetical Poetical – 2

O

## **O**ld Hamster Jam

We used to own a hamster who was very old,
One day he died and we all cried,
No furry friend to hold.

We all were very sad that he had passed away,
But then I knew just what to do,
Upon that very day.

I took the little hamster, whom we all called Dan,
Removed his skin, and then placed him,
Inside a new saucepan.

Dan was tough to melt and we had to push and ram,
But very soon, upon the spoon,
We found ourselves with jam.

We then made some toast and spread the jam upon it,
We'd made our tea, but deary me,
That jam tasted horrid.

I took the jam and threw it out into the garden
But through the night, in the moonlight,
It began to harden.

Next day we all looked outside, sniffing with our noses,
And all around, all of the ground,
Was covered all with roses.

We blinked our eyes upon the view which swam and swam,
We would have bet, you'd always get
Tulips from hamster jam.

~~~~~

## **O**rigami

Origami, origami, origami, origami:
A word you can say fourfold.
There are thousands of things you can make
from one sheet -
Its uses are so manifold!

~ ~ ~ ~ ~

## **O**xygen

Let's thank the stars that oxygen
Can't travel fast but goes quite slow,
For if it travelled faster then
You couldn't catch your breath, oh no!

~ ~ ~ ~ ~

Steve Morley  Alphabetical Poetical – 2

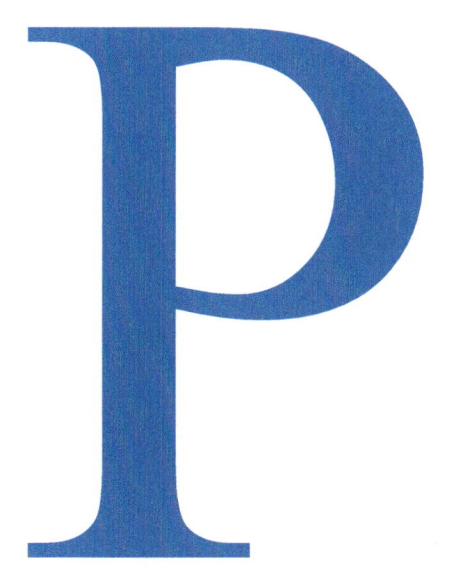

P

## Piranha Boomerang

I once owned a piranha fish
That was bad in a nasty way
I stuck it to a boomerang
And I tried to throw it away
But as it left my fingertips
An awful thought came to fright me –
That pretty soon this dreadful fish
Would be coming back to bite me.

~ ~ ~ ~ ~

## Plastic Duck

My plastic duck is filthy
I don't know where he's been
I put him in the bath with me
And now he's squeaky clean

~ ~ ~ ~ ~

## **P**ity The Birds

Pity if you will, the stork,
Who has to be most shrewish,
He must be careful in his work
Because the baby's newish

Pity if you will, the cock
Whose crow could be much calmer,
For if he's calm at six o'clock
He will not wake the farmer.

Pity please the goose, I beg,
Who really wants a daughter,
For when she lays that monstrous egg
Her eyes begin to water.

Pity, if you will, the birds
Who cannot ever fly,
What's the use of being a bird
If you can't look down from high?

~ ~ ~ ~ ~

Steve Morley	Alphabetical Poetical – 2

## **Question**

I thought, when asked the question:
'What's the smallest British bird?'
The answer was the Finch.
Or so, that's what I'd heard.
But then, my friend, he said to me,
"There's one smaller than the Finch,
Which is the seldom heard
Lesser-spotted Halfinch."

But now I have a problem,
I think both of us are wrong.
Could you guess the smallest
By sight or by its song?
So I looked in my bird book,
On a shelf, sat in its nest,
And it said the smallest
Is, of course, the Goldcrest.

~ ~ ~ ~ ~

**FACT: The goldcrest is so small it weighs almost exactly the same as a 20p piece.**

## Question of the Future

A question once was put to me,
By a silly old friend of mine,
"What would you like said about you
In around two hundred years' time?"

Now this was not a question that I
Ever thought I'd have to engage,
But I said I'd like them to say,
"My word, he looks good for his age!"

~~~~~

## Quink

Have you ever done a Quink?
It's not what you might think
It's when you close one eye very fast
Much quicker than a wink.

~~~~~

Steve Morley	Alphabetical Poetical – 2

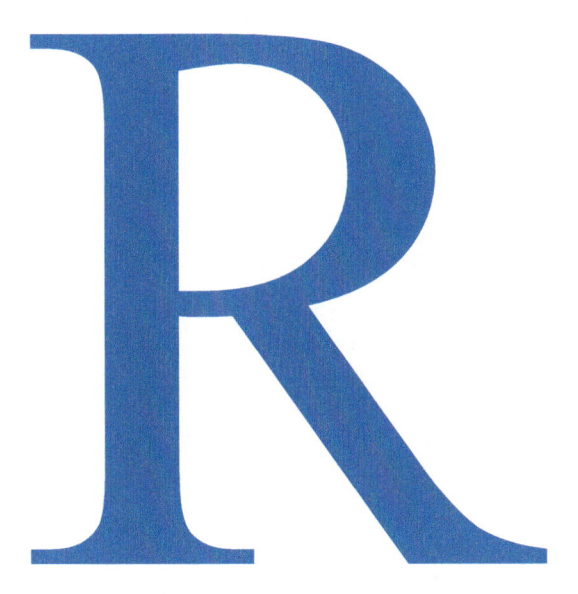

R

## **R**acing Toilet

I knew a racing driver
Who owned a racing circuit
And as he didn't like it
He called it The Racing Toilet.

He used to drive me round it
For hours that wouldn't end
And as he was so boring
It would drive me around the bend.

~ ~ ~ ~ ~

## **R**atel

Do not have a fight with the ratel
For the end of it might well be fatal.
And stay far away if a cadger you be,
For this fierce honey badger won't lend you 10p.

~ ~ ~ ~ ~

## **R**ebecca

There was a young girl called Rebecca,
Who thought that she was a woodpecker,
She went to a wood,
And pecked all she could,
Till the proper woodpeckers did deck her

~ ~ ~ ~ ~

Steve Morley    Alphabetical Poetical – 2

S

## **S**erial Cuddler

I'm a serial cuddler, cuddler,
A serial cuddler – me!
      I cuddle my mam and I cuddle my gran
      And I cuddle my dad for free.

I'm a serial cuddler, cuddler,
A serial cuddler – me!
      I cuddle the dog when he's been for a jog
      And I cuddle my daft dog's flea.

I'm a serial cuddler, cuddler,
A serial cuddler – me!
      I cuddle the rat that's been caught by cat
      And I cuddle the back yard tree.

I'm a serial cuddler, cuddler,
A serial cuddler – me!
      I cuddle the horse and the cow, of course,
      And I cuddle the beans for tea.

I'm a serial cuddler, cuddler,
A serial cuddler – me!
      I cuddle the snails that live on the whales
      And I cuddle the great North Sea.

I'm a serial cuddler, cuddler,
A serial cuddler – me!
      I cuddle the earth with my arms round its girth
      That's the whole of the world, you see.

I'm a serial cuddler, cuddler,
A serial cuddler – me!
    I cuddle Mars then put my arms round the stars,
    And the universe cuddles me.

~ ~ ~ ~ ~

## Sizzling Sausages

Sizzling sausages,
I wonder where the porridge is?
We always eat our porridges
Before we have our sausages.

~ ~ ~ ~ ~

## Stroked Spiders

A scientific fact, we're told,
By scientists, both young and old,
Is, if you can, a spider hold,
And stroke its back, it will go bald.

As grapes are grapes and figs are figs,
And geese are geese and pigs are pigs,
Stroked spiders never dance their jigs
Unless they're wearing brand new wigs.

~ ~ ~ ~ ~

Steve Morley    Alphabetical Poetical – 2

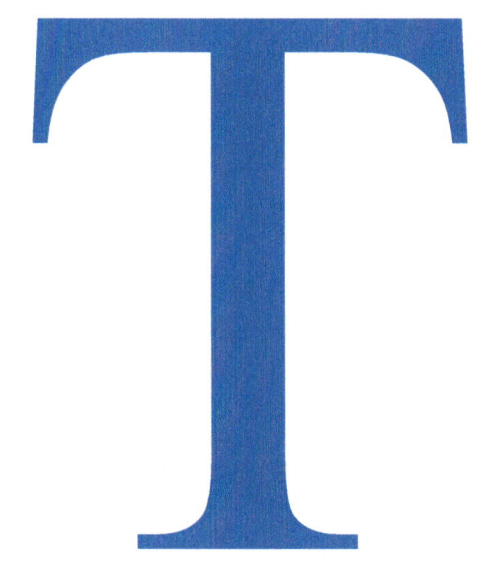

T

## T-H Words

Unlucky things are Spelling birds
Constantly attacked by T-H words
They fend off words like 'This' and 'There'
But quite often get caught unaware
Even if they sit there humming
They always fail to see 'That' coming.

~ ~ ~ ~ ~

## Time Traveller

When I met him at the station,
He said he was a traveller in time.
When I asked him what he meant, he said:
"I just travelled in the ten past nine."

~ ~ ~ ~ ~

## Tell Us A Story Mammy

Tell us a story Mammy,
Tell to us a tale,
Tell us all about the big white whale.
Was he a monster Mammy
With a big tail?
Tell us Mammy all about the big white whale.

Tell us a story Mammy,
Tell us of the air,
Tell us all about the things up there.
Are they right scary Mammy
Covered with hair?
Tell us Mammy all about the things up there.

Tell us a story Mammy,
Tell us of the sea,
Tell us all about what we might see.
Is it right awful Mammy
Dark as can be?
Tell us Mammy all about what we might see.

Tell us a story Mammy,
Tell to us a yarn,
Tell us all about the socks you darn.
Are they right smelly Mammy,
Knitted with yarn?
Tell us Mammy all about the socks you darn.

Tell us a story Mammy,
You can make it so,
Tell us all about where we might go.
Will we travel far Mammy,
Do you not know?
Tell us Mammy all about where we might go.

Tell us a story Mammy,
Tell of things to come,
Tell us all about what we'll become.
Will we be happy Mammy,
Will we be glum?
Tell us all about it Mammy,
Tell us all about it Mammy,
Please tell us about it Mammy,
Tell us Mammy all about what we'll become.

~ ~ ~ ~ ~

Steve Morley                    Alphabetical Poetical – 2

U

## **U**gandan Girl

There was a young girl from Uganda,
Who decided her geese should be blander.
She worked hard all day
Taking sweetness away,
Till she fell in love with a gander.

~~~~~

## **U**mbrella

I have in my hands an old umbrella
I bought it from a little old feller,
It's black on the outside but within coloured yeller,
She's my pride and joy and I'm never gonna sell 'er.

~~~~~

## **U**ncle Dennis

My uncle Dennis
Was killed playing tennis
When he fell after slipping on ice.
I would like to say, when we sent him away,
His service was all very nice.

~~~~~

Steve Morley     Alphabetical Poetical – 2

V

## Vain Money Waster

There was a young lady so vain,
She would never be seen in the rain,
And such was her haste
That she tended to waste
All her money which went down the drain.

~ ~ ~ ~ ~

## Very Deep Sea

I always love the ocean, me,
I love to take the plunge,
But how much deeper would it be,
If it lacked every sponge?

~ ~ ~ ~ ~

## **V**egetable Men

They told me of the vegetable men,
Of how they march in November,
When the nights are as crisp as lettuce
And carrots fresh from the ground.

They told me of their vegetable legs,
Of how they ran to remember
Where they had left their vegetable heads
And bellies, cabbagey round.

They told me if you got in the way
Of the vegetables in November,
They'd think of you as one of their own,
And take you down underground.

Down to where all the vegetable men
Weather the cold of December,
And hope that they will rise up again,
Once more when Spring comes around.

~ ~ ~ ~ ~

Steve Morley    Alphabetical Poetical – 2

W

## **W**hale **W**arning

Just the other day as I was walking down the road,
I met a whale who told me he was going to explode.
So I ran along the street telling those I know:
"There is no doubt about it,
I'll shout it and I'll spout it,
Get yourselves inside because this whale is going to blow!"

~ ~ ~ ~ ~

## **W**hen My Voice Broke

When my voice broke...

                  ...I was taking part...

In a concert...

                  ...at the Sacred Heart...

I was to be...

                  ...one of the three kings...

One of the three...

                  ...soloists that sings...

When my voice broke...

                  ...I was badly shocked...

The other kings...

                  ...broadly smiled and mocked...

My voice it cracked...

                  ...like an old jam jar...

Miserable un...

                  …happy Balthazar...

~ ~ ~ ~ ~

## Why, Oh – Why, Oh

Why, oh – why, oh,
Do I do those things, oh,
That they tell me are a no-no?

Why, oh – why, oh,
When I write out 'why, oh – why, oh',
Does it spell out the word 'yo-yo'?

~ ~ ~ ~ ~

Steve Morley    Alphabetical Poetical – 2

X

# X

X is a Roman numeral,
I use it now and then,
Sometimes it helps me mark the spot,
Sometimes it equals ten.
Sometimes it shows me when I'm wrong,
Sometimes it crosses out
A poem that I'm working on
Which I just can't work out.
Sometimes it helps me multiply,
Sometimes it's just a kiss
Placed at the bottom of a card
Sent to the ones I miss.

~ ~ ~ ~ ~

## X-Ray

I used to know a man whose name was Ray,
Who broke his leg and so they X-rayed Ray.
They told him when would be his X-ray day,
But just before, poor Ray, he passed away.
We think about poor Ray from day to day,
And when we do, we speak about ex-Ray.

~ ~ ~ ~ ~

## Xebec

A xebec was an old sailing ship
That was once sailed by old corsairs
Now sailors are known to use coarse words
But not as coarse as old corsairs

~ ~ ~ ~ ~

Steve Morley  Alphabetical Poetical – 2

Y

## **Y**oobub

The Yoobub is a thingumybob,
A thingumybob with snoo,
The Yoobub is a whatsumycall
That should be in a zoo.

The Yoobub is a howdoyousay,
A howdoyousay with snay,
The Yoobub is a whichumything
That stays out night and day.

The Youbub is a whatyummysmell.
A whatyummysmell with snork,
The Yoobub is a knowwhatImean,
That eats with knife and fork.

The Yoobub is a whatsitawhat,
A whatsitawhat with sweak,
The Yoobub is a whatsthatagain,
That still declines to speak.

The Yoobub is a seenembefore,
A seenembefore with splance.
The Yoobub is a flippertyflap,
That loves to flirt and dance.

The Yoobub is a howdoyoudo,
A howdoyoudo with splack,
The Yoobub is a whereishenow,
I hope that he comes back.

~ ~ ~ ~ ~

### **You Know It Makes Sense**

Come down from that ladder and eat up your tea,
If you break your both legs don't come running to me.

Don't play with those scissors, don't make me shout it,
If you cut off your tongue don't tell me about it.

Don't mess with that needle, it's sharp don't you see,
If you poke out your eyes don't come looking for me.

Don't climb, play or meddle, you're making me tense,
You know what I'm saying...
...you know it makes sense.

~ ~ ~ ~ ~

### **Younger**

The man said to me, "Here's a photograph,
It's of me when I was younger."
I said, "But every photograph of you,
Is of you when you were younger."

~ ~ ~ ~ ~

Steve Morley                    Alphabetical Poetical – 2

# Z

## **Z**ealous Photographer

He went to take a photograph
Of a massive crocodile,
Whose jaws began to open wide…
In the biggest…ever…smile.

And so he moved much closer to
That gargantuan reptile,
While looking through the camera lens…
And the croc…maintained…its smile.

Then as he poked his head inside,
Past the rows of teeth and smile,
A glint appeared within its eye…
A snap-happy…croc…o…dile!

~ ~ ~ ~ ~

## Zanzi Bar

I once went to visit a Zanzi bar,
Where they served specialist zanzis.
A splash of the zans would give it its ziz
Much better by far than cranberries.

~~~~~

## Zappy

My baby brother Zappy,
Is the cutest little chappie
Especially when he's had enough to eat
And when it all comes out
You should hear him shout
He's the greatest happy-clappy Zappy in a nappy
You'd ever want to meet!

~~~~~

**Also Available from Amazon**

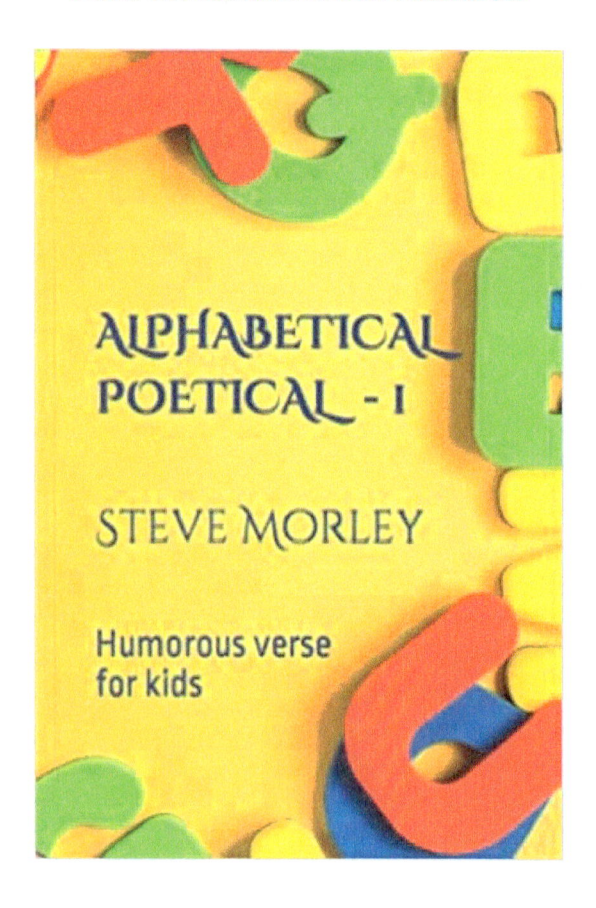

# Also Available from Amazon

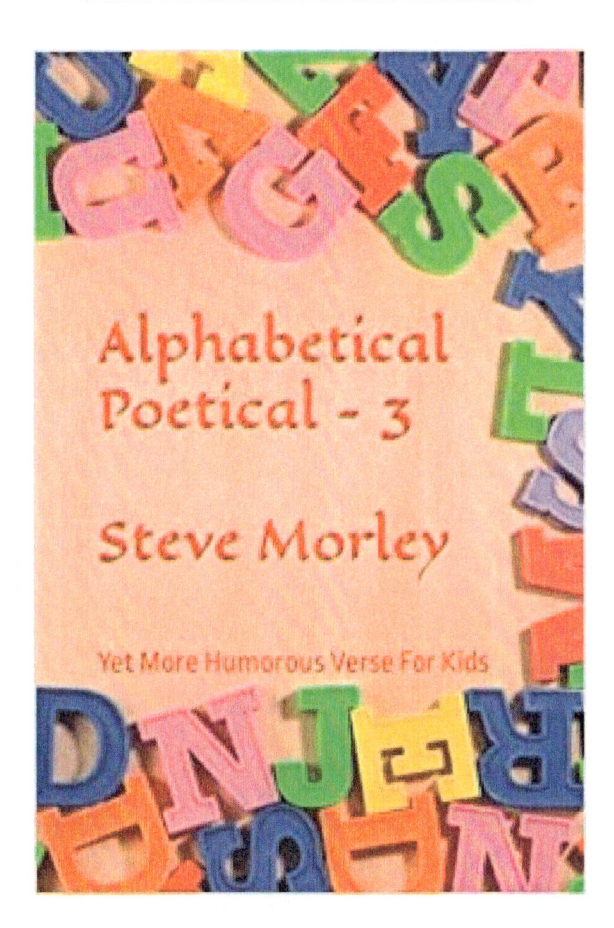

## Alphabetical Poetical - 3

### Steve Morley

Yet More Humorous Verse For Kids

**Also Available from Amazon**

# Alphabetical Poetical

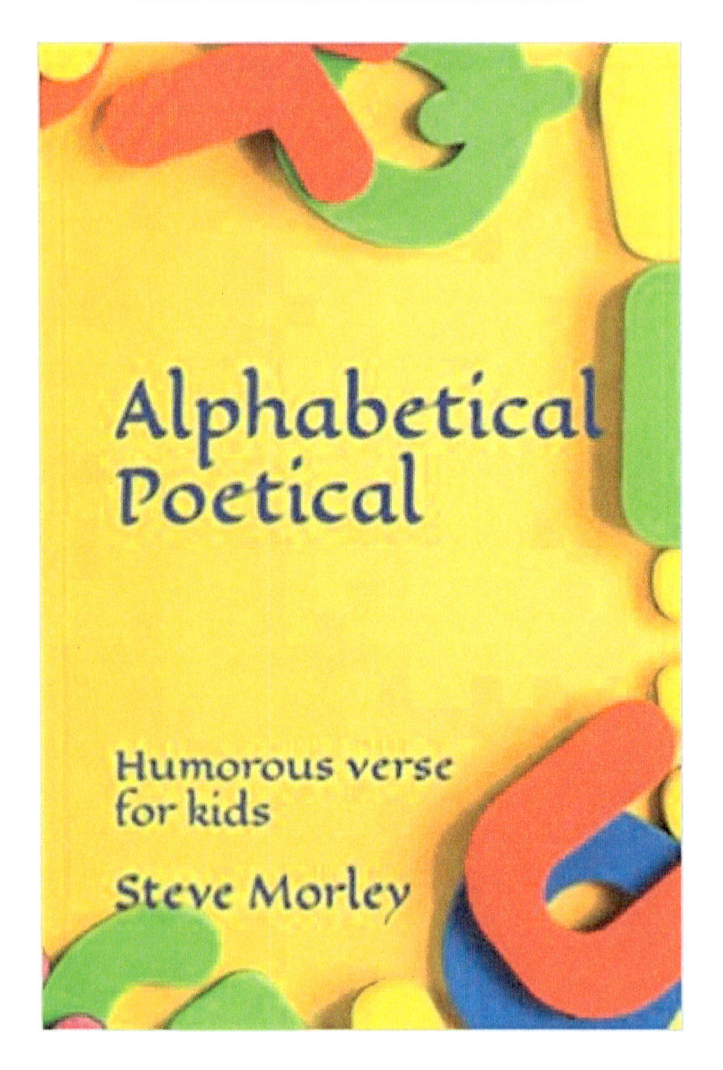

Humorous verse for kids

Steve Morley

Alphabetical Poetical books 1, 2 & 3 now combined in this one volume.

# Also Available from Amazon

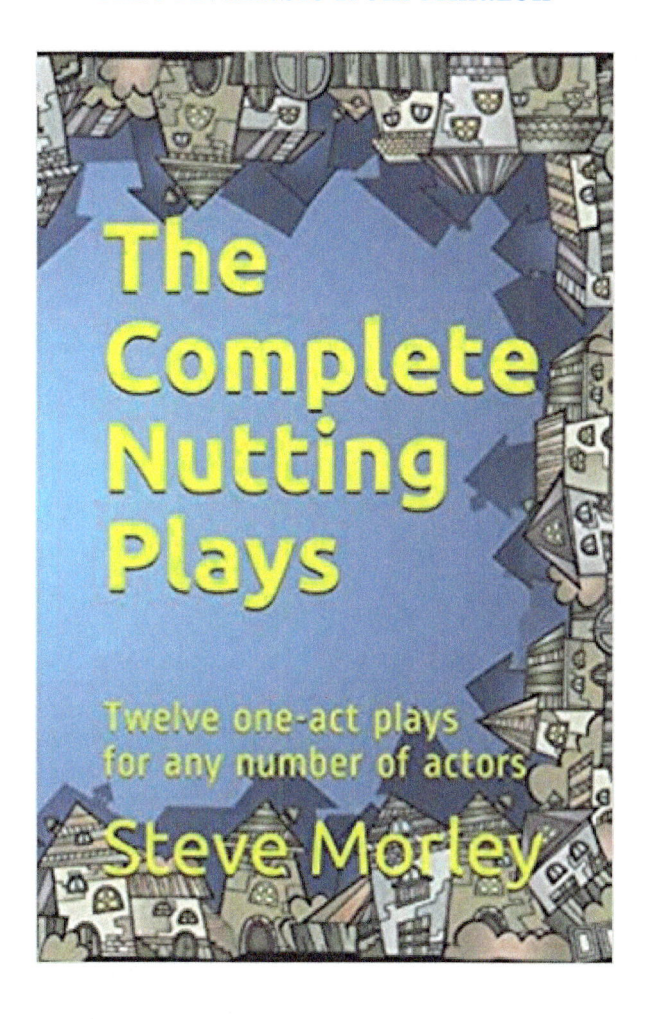

## The Complete Nutting Plays

Twelve one-act plays for any number of actors

Steve Morley

Nutting is a town where everybody lives ordinary lives in an extraordinary way, and where everyone who lives there is known as a Nutter.

Printed in Great Britain
by Amazon